DOLLS

written by
Judy Ann Sadler

illustrated by Marilyn Mets

KIDS CAN PRESS LTD.
Toronto

To my best-loved dolls of all,
Carly, Denby and Emily

Canadian Cataloguing in Publication Data

Sadler, Judy Ann, 1959–
Dolls

(Kids Can Easy Crafts)
ISBN 1-55074-130-6

1. Dollmaking — Juvenile literature. 2. Dollmaking.
3. Handicrafts — Juvenile literature. I. Mets, Marilyn.
II. Title. III. Series.

TT175.S23 1993 j745.592'21 C92-094484-1

Many designations used by manufacturers and sellers to distinguish their products are claimed as trademarks. Where those designations appear in this book and Kids Can Press Ltd. was aware of a trademark claim, the designations have been printed in initial capital letters (i.e., Popsicle).

Neither the Publisher nor the Author shall be liable for any damage which may be caused or sustained as a result of the conduct of any of the activities in this book, from not specifically following instructions or conducting the activities without proper supervision, or from ignoring the cautions contained in the text.

Kids Can Press Ltd.
29 Birch Avenue
Toronto, Ontario, Canada
M4V 1E2

Edited by Laurie Wark
Designed by Nancy Ruth Jackson
Printed and bound in Hong Kong
93 0 9 8 7 6 5 4 3

CONTENTS

GETTING STARTED

Did you know that there's a pal in your pencil case? A buddy in the button box? There are dolls in the making all around you. What do you get when you twist together pipe cleaners, add a bead, roly eyes and a bowtie? A playmate ready for a party! How about when you wrap a scrap of fabric around a stone? A rock-a-bye baby, of course! Gather together buttons, beads, bits of felt, yarn, fabric and pipe cleaners. You likely have lots of doll materials around your home; look for others in fabric and craft supply stores. Twist, bend, wrap and glue, and you're on your way to making dolls that magically become small friends. Happy dollmaking!

pipe cleaners (chenille stems) They come in two lengths:

short - 15 cm (6 inches)
long - 30 cm (12 inches)

If short pipe cleaners are called for and you have long ones, simply cut or bend them in half.

beads You can find beads in a variety of colours and shapes. Look for old necklaces at garage and junk sales. Wooden beads are perfect for doll heads. Use tiny beads to decorate doll clothes and make doll faces.

roly eyes These come in many colours and sizes at craft stores. They add a fun look to your doll.

fabric Look in your rag box for fabric scraps or parts of clothing not worn out. Fabric stores have remnant bins where you can find small pieces of fabric at bargain prices. Bandannas are good, too.

scissors You'll need scissors sharp enough to cut fabric, yarn and felt, and strong enough to cut pipe cleaners. Ask an adult for help when you're cutting. If you have pinking shears, use them when you cut fabric. They leave a zigzag edge that will not fray. If you don't have pinking shears, spread glue along fabric edges to help prevent fraying.

stuffing Some dolls in this book need a little stuffing. You can use polyester fibre fill stuffing, clean soft rags, old pantyhose or tissue.

paint Acrylic paint is excellent for doll faces. It cleans up with soap and water.

glue Use good-quality, clear-drying white glue.

other stuff Yarn, lace, ribbon, buttons, felt, sequins, spools, nuts, feathers, acorns, apple seeds, construction paper and noodles can all be used for dollmaking.

Face

eyes To make eyes, use tiny beads, roly eyes, bits of felt or construction paper. To paint eyes, dip a toothpick or the wrong end of a fine paintbrush into paint and dab it onto the face.

nose Use a tiny bead, felt, construction paper or paint for a nose. Because some of the dolls are very small, you may find that there is no room for a nose.

mouth Make a mouth by painting one with a fine paintbrush, gluing a piece of string into a smile or by using felt or construction paper. Make a surprised mouth by gluing on a little round bead.

Hair

ponytail Wind yarn around your hand or a piece of cardboard three or four times. Tie it into a knot near the front to make the hair look like bangs and a ponytail. A ponytail works well on a bead head because you can glue it on so that the knot sits down a little in the bead's hole.

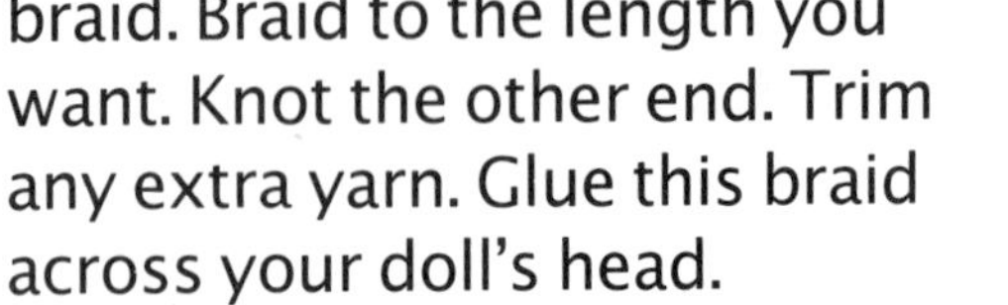

braids Cut three or more pieces of yarn and knot them together at one end. Tuck the knot under something heavy or ask someone to hold onto it while you braid. Braid to the length you want. Knot the other end. Trim any extra yarn. Glue this braid across your doll's head.

short fuzzy hair Cut yarn into little pieces and pile them on your work table. Spread glue on your doll's head and dip it into the yarn bits. Gently pat the bits down.

frizzy hair Cut some strands of yarn and glue them side by side across your doll's head. Untwist each strand for a frizzy look.

short hair Cut short pieces of yarn and glue them side by side across your doll's head.

curly hair Tightly wind crochet cotton or embroidery floss around a toothpick for tight curls or a pencil or knitting needle for looser curls. Tie or tape the ends. Do not overlap the floss as you wind. Soak it in water and let it dry overnight. Gently glue the curls to your doll's head.

Accessories

hats Acorn "cups" make wonderful caps. Also, try buttons, felt, paper, bread-bag tags or fabric. For a royal look, shape a crown out of a tinsel pipe cleaner.

capes Cut out a rectangle of felt. Fold over one long edge. Cut slits in it. Weave a ribbon or string through the slits. Add gold trim for royal dolls, a felt "S" for super-dolls or any other trim you like.

other stuff Shape a tiny pair of glasses out of wire. Make a walking stick from a twig. How about earrings and a necklace of tiny beads? Use a paper doily for a dress or skirt. Make small paper books or toothpick hockey sticks, and create furniture out of empty spools and little boxes.

PAPER DOLL STRINGS

THINGS YOU NEED:

1 Fan-fold your paper wide enough to draw a doll on it.

2 Draw a doll shape on the folded paper, making sure that the arms and feet go off the edges.

3 With the paper still folded, cut out the doll shape. Unfold and admire!

Fun ideas to try

To make a longer doll string, use wrapping paper or newsprint from a roll. Instead of fan-folding the paper to fit one doll shape, fold it wide enough to fit two.

PEANUT BUDDIES

THINGS YOU NEED:

1. Use roly eyes, tiny beads, bits of felt or paper for the eyes. Glue them in place.

2. Finish the face using markers, felt, paper or paint. Try an apple seed for the nose.

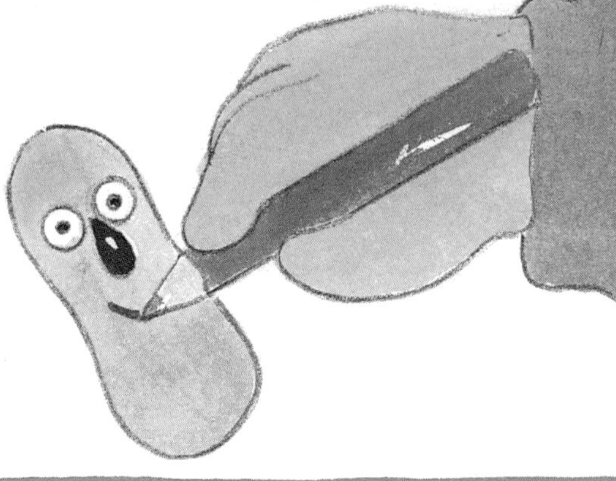

3. Give your peanut buddy a hairstyle, a bowtie or buttons.

Fun ideas to try

- Make a peanut stand by cutting a circle out of lightweight cardboard. Glue it onto the bottom of your peanut buddy.
- Glue a magnetic strip to the back of your peanut buddy.

ROCK-A-BYE BABY

THINGS YOU NEED:

1 Put a line of glue around the top of your stone, and place the lace over the glue.

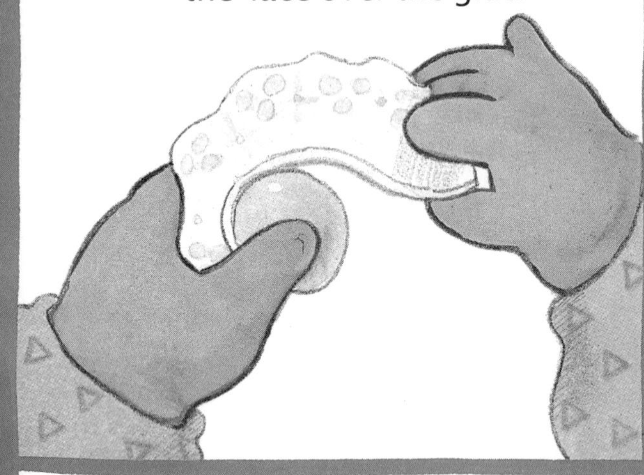

2 Cut a rectangle of fabric. Fold down one long edge of the rectangle.

3 Wrap the blanket around the stone so that it covers the lace ends and so there are no unfinished edges showing. Glue it in place.

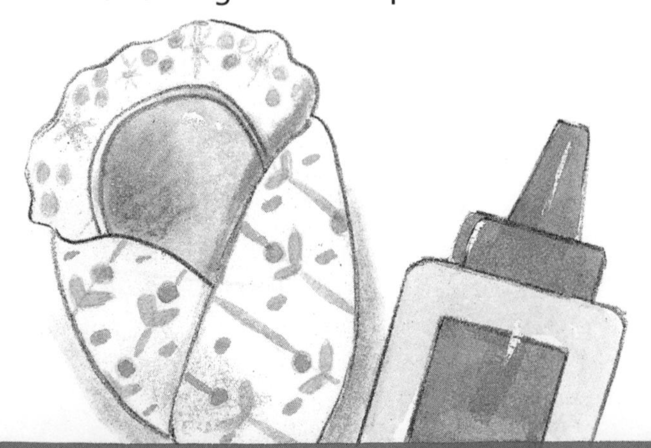

4 Give your rock-a-bye baby a simple face.

PENCIL PALS

THINGS YOU NEED:

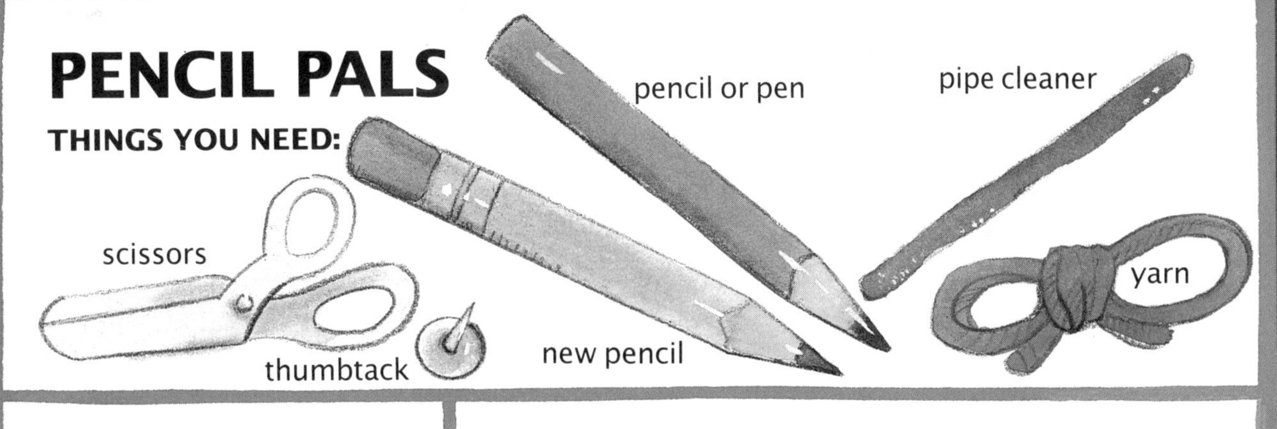

1 Cut three pieces of yarn and arrange them in a hairstyle.

2 Use the thumbtack to hold the hair in place on the pencil eraser.

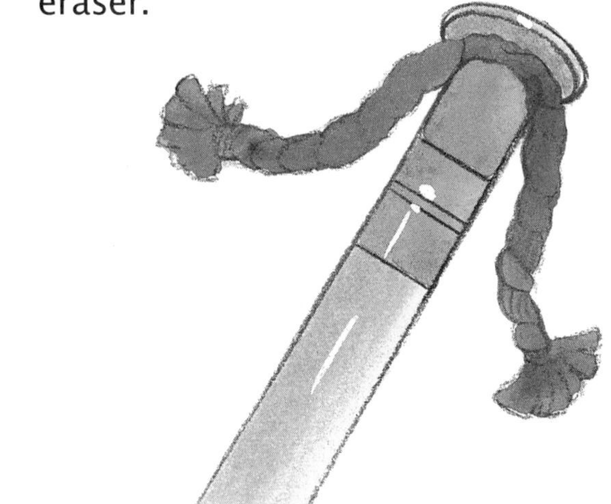

3 Draw a face on the eraser.

4 Wrap the pipe cleaner around your pencil . Twist it twice at the back and bring the ends to the front for arms. Trim them and fold them inward for hands.

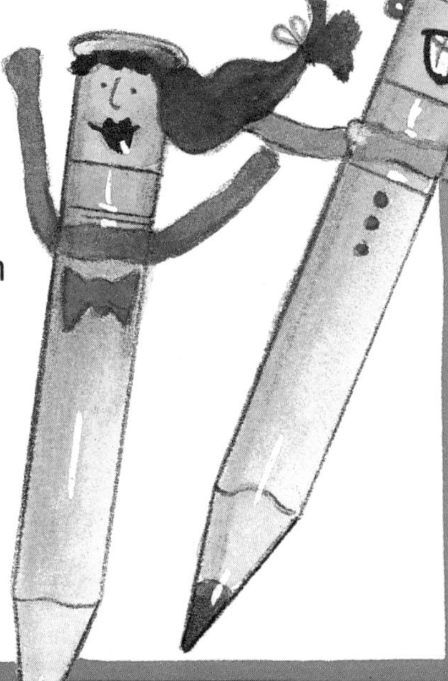

BEAD BUDDIES

THINGS YOU NEED:

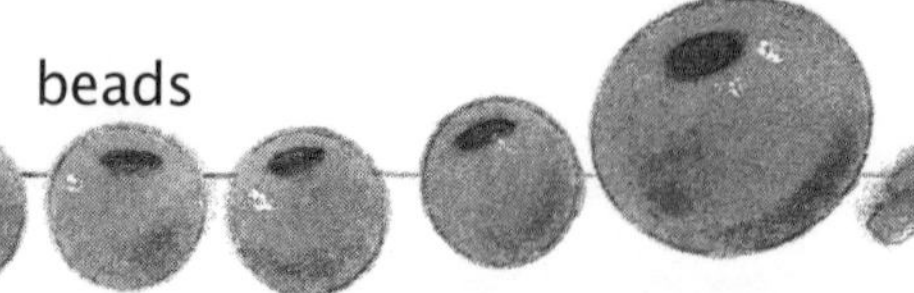

1 Hold two pipe cleaners side by side. If the large bead has a big hole, bend down the tops of the pipe cleaners. Put glue on this bent-down part and slide it into the bead. (If your bead has a small hole, you don't need to bend the pipe cleaners.)

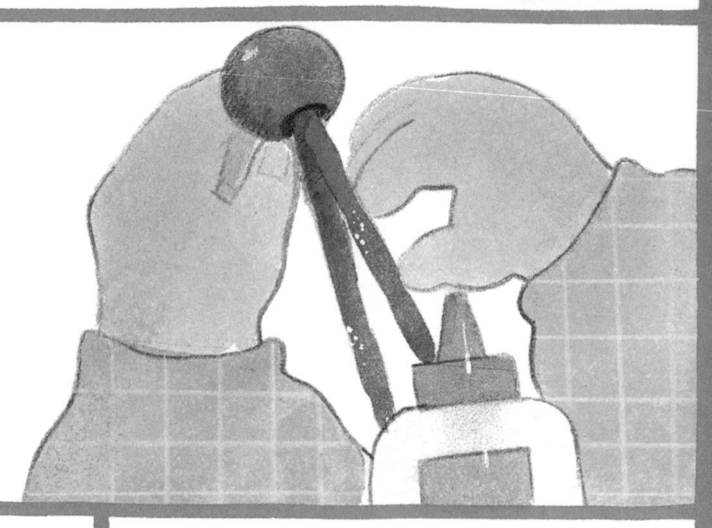

2 For arms, hold the third pipe cleaner behind the body pipe cleaners. Make one arm a little longer than the other.

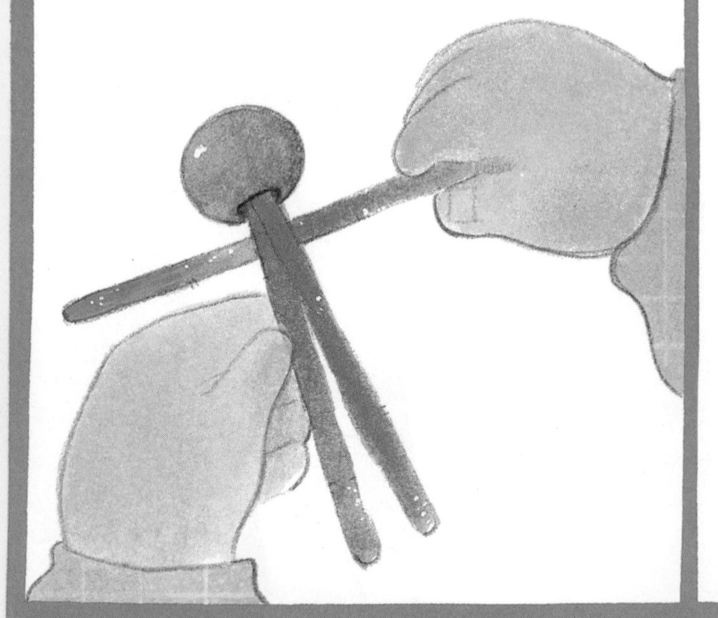

3 Tightly wrap the longer arm around the body twice and return it to the arm position.

4 Loosely thread beads onto the arms. When you get near the end of each arm, bend the pipe cleaner to look like hands.

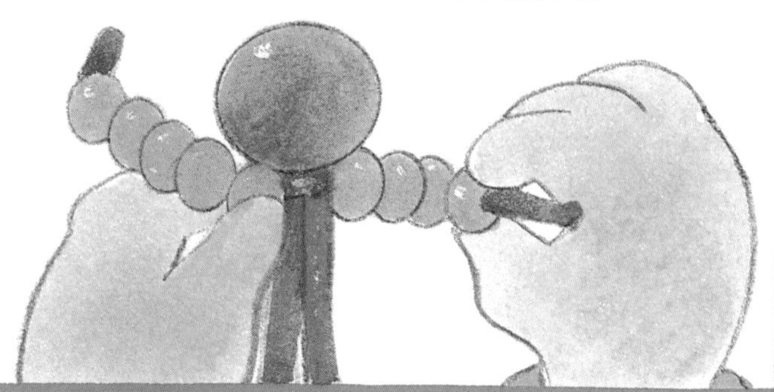

5 Thread a few beads up both pipe cleaners to make the body.

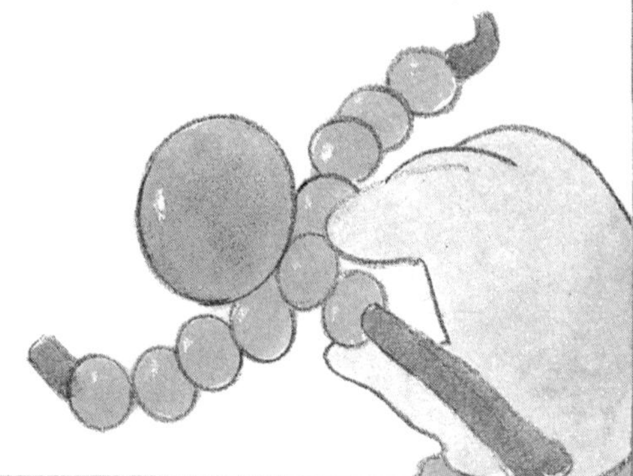

6 Separate the pipe cleaners into two legs. Loosely thread beads onto each one. Bend the ends to make feet.

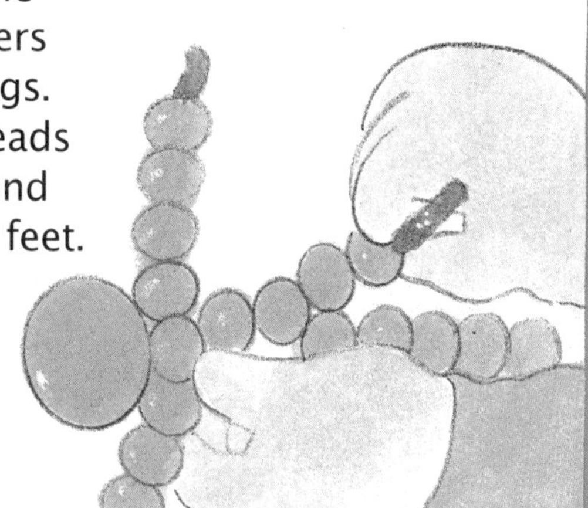

7 Give your doll a face and hairstyle.

Fun ideas to try

❤ To make a skirt, cut a circle out of felt or fabric. Cut a tiny hole in the centre. Before beading the legs, thread the skirt up to the middle. Bead the legs to keep the skirt in place.

BUTTON BUDDIES

THINGS YOU NEED:

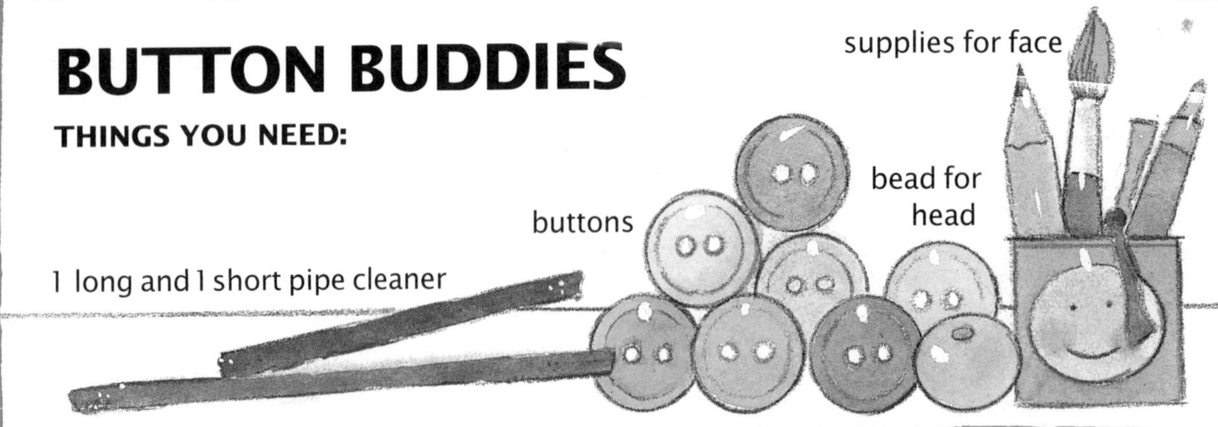

1 Fold the long pipe cleaner in half and thread a button onto it. The button is your doll's hat.

2 Put the bead head onto the pipe cleaner.

3 Thread buttons onto the pipe cleaner to make your doll's body. Leave enough pipe cleaner for the legs.

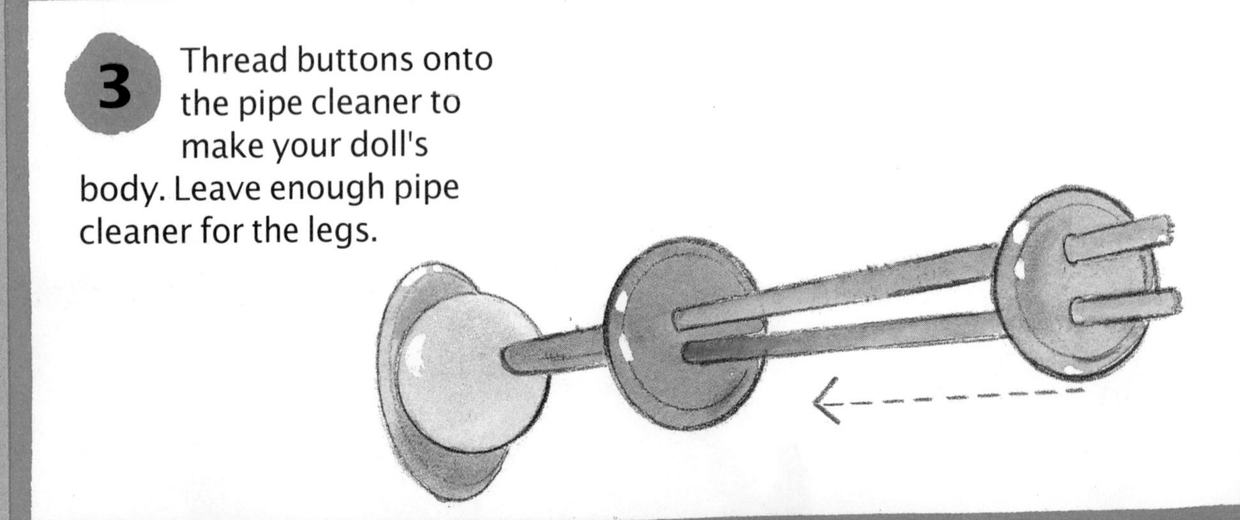

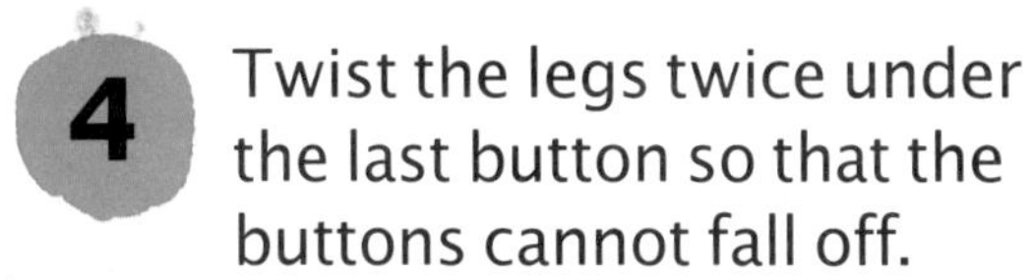

4 Twist the legs twice under the last button so that the buttons cannot fall off.

5 To make arms, wind the short pipe cleaner between the second and third buttons.

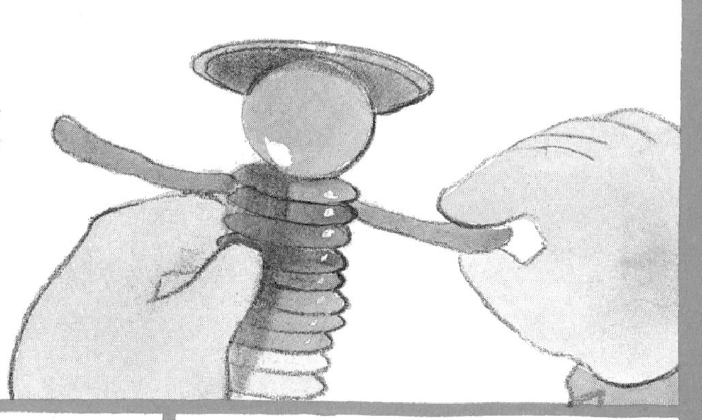

6 Fold back the ends of the pipe cleaners to make hands and feet.

7 Give your button buddy a face.

Fun ideas to try

- Instead of using buttons for the body, use an empty thread spool. Use a button hat and a button above and below the spool.
- Run a ribbon under the pipe cleaner on top of your doll's button hat to hang it up.
- Make a button baby by using shorter pipe cleaner pieces and little buttons.

WEE WALNUTS

THINGS YOU NEED:

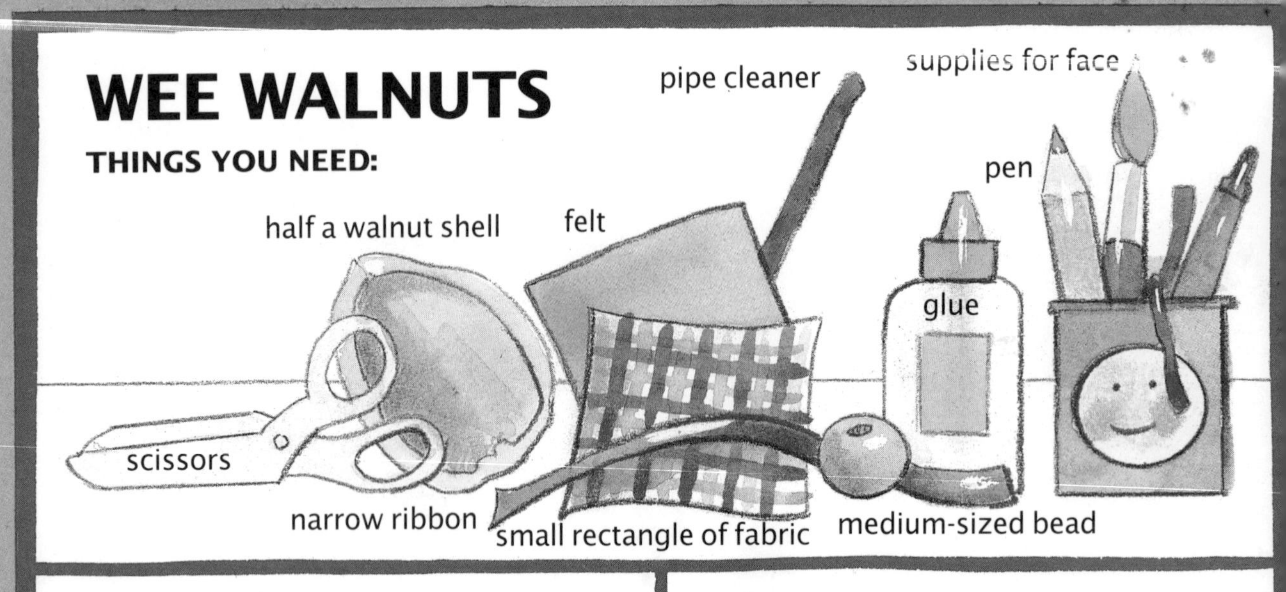

1 Draw a circle a little bigger than the walnut shell on the felt. Cut it out.

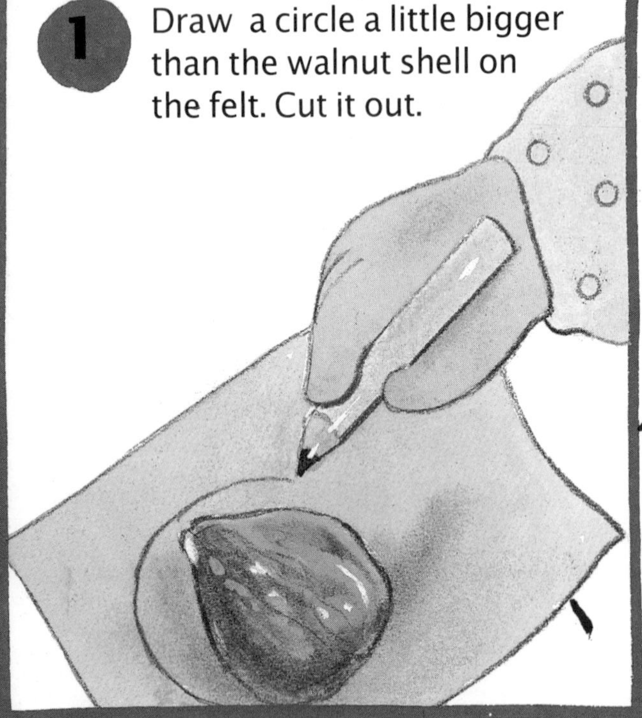

2 Squirt glue into the walnut shell. Press the centre of the ribbon and the felt circle into the glue.

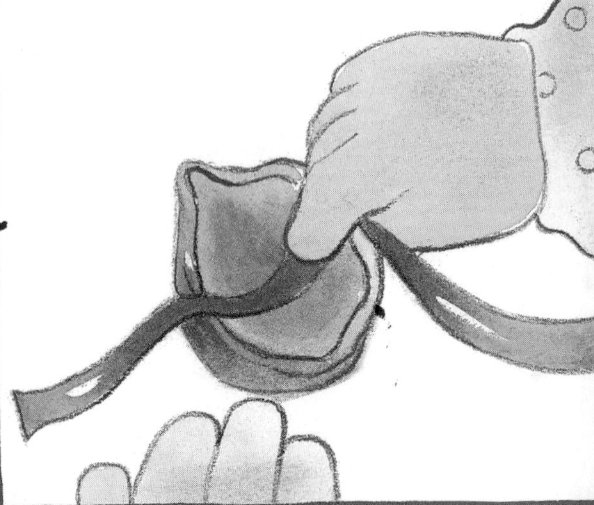

3 Cut a piece of pipe cleaner a little shorter than the inside of the walnut shell. Put a drop of glue on the end of it and slide it into the bead.

4 Place the rectangle of fabric right side down on the table. Fold over a long edge. Lightly glue it down.

5 Run a line of glue all around the bead. Place the folded edge of the fabric over the bead and pinch it together under the chin.

6 Fold the fabric blanket up halfway from the bottom. Fold it up again, under your walnut baby's chin. Wrap the side pieces of the blanket around to the back and glue them in place.

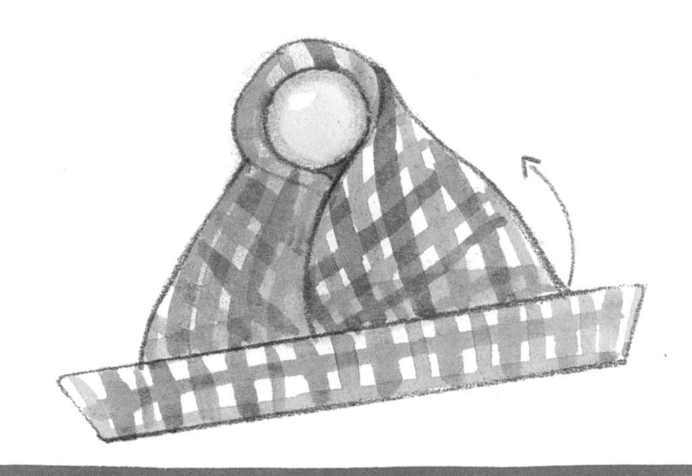

7 Squirt glue onto the felt in the walnut. Tuck your baby doll in, with the head at the pointed end of the shell.

8 Give your baby doll a simple face. Tie the ends of the ribbon together and hang it up.

PEG PEOPLE

THINGS YOU NEED:

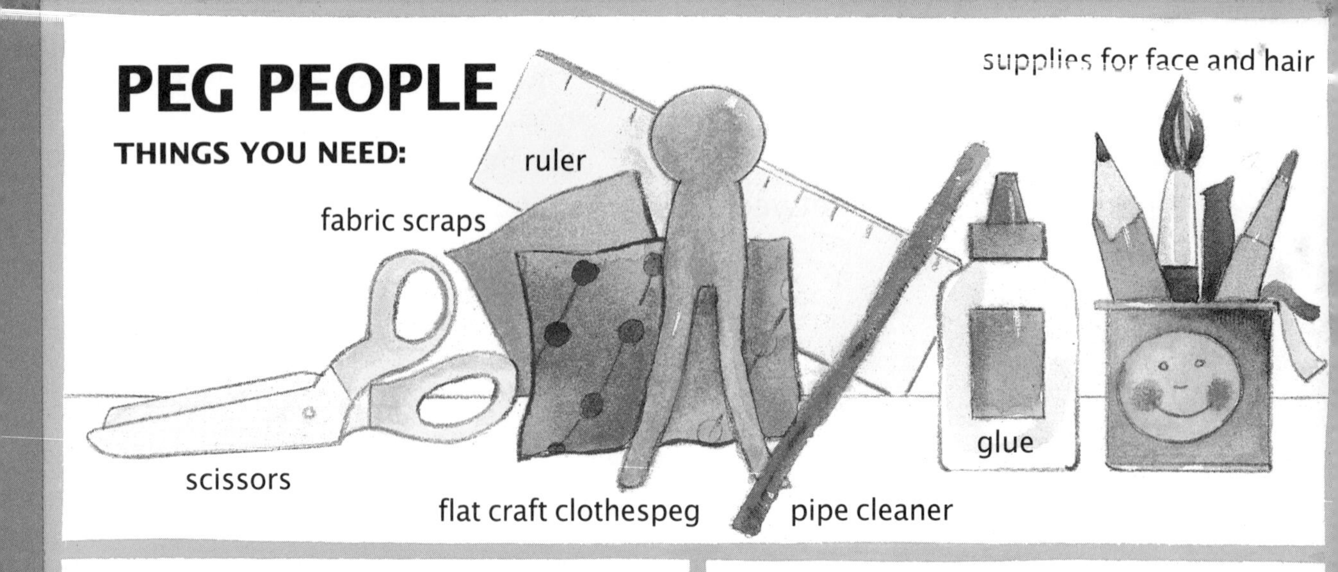

1 Cut a rectangle of fabric 3 cm x 6 cm (1¼ inches x 2¼ inches). This will be your doll's shirt.

2 Cut a 7 cm x 7 cm (3 inches x 3 inches) square of fabric. This will be your doll's pants.

3 Fold down one long edge of the shirt fabric. Wrap the fabric around your doll with the folded edge at your doll's neck. Glue it closed at the back.

4 Spread glue all over your doll's legs.

5 Fold down one edge of the pants fabric. Wrap this edge around your doll's waist and glue it at the back. Poke the fabric in between the doll's legs so it looks like pants.

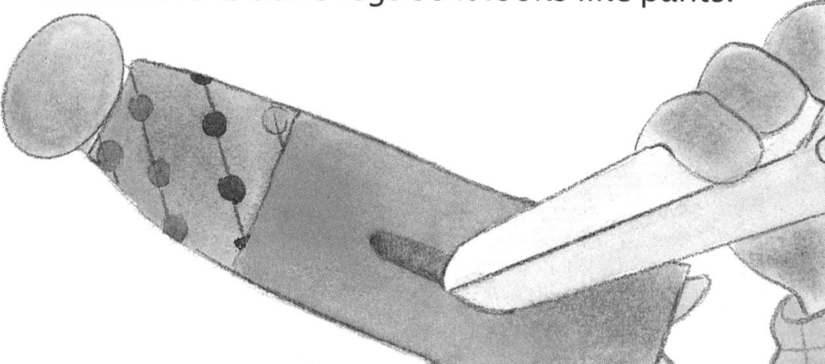

6 Wrap the pipe cleaner around your doll's waist for a belt. Twist the ends together twice at the back and bring them to the front for arms.

7 Finish your peg person with a face and hairstyle.

Fun ideas to try

- If you want a dress for your doll, cut a circle out of fabric. Use a small bowl as a guide. Make a slit in the centre. Bring the dress up over the doll's legs to its neck. Use a pipe cleaner as a belt and arms, as usual.

YARN DOLL

THINGS YOU NEED:

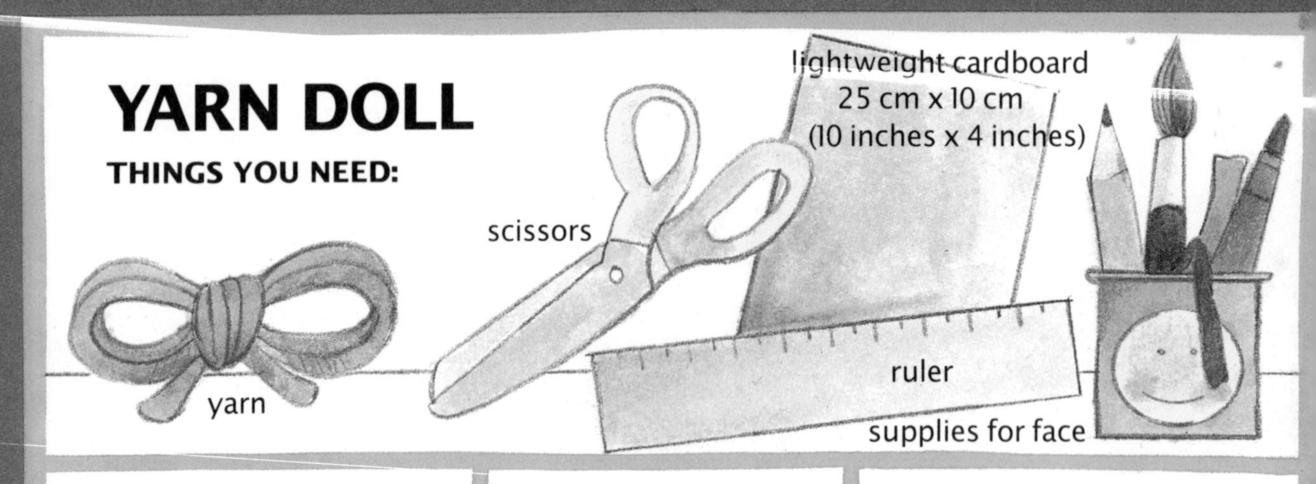

1 Wind the yarn around the cardboard about 20 times for thick yarn or 50 times for thin yarn.

2 Gently slide the yarn off the cardboard.

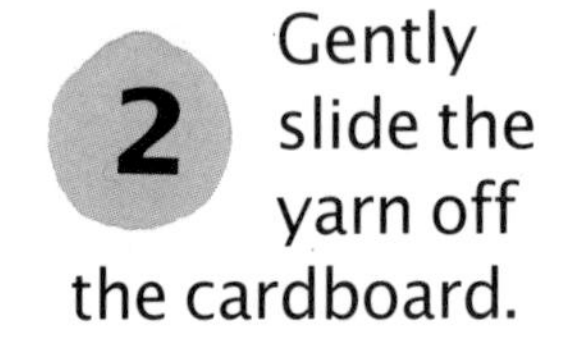

3 To make the hair, cut a piece of yarn about 50 cm (20 inches) long, and tie it snugly a little down from the top. Let the ends hang down the back.

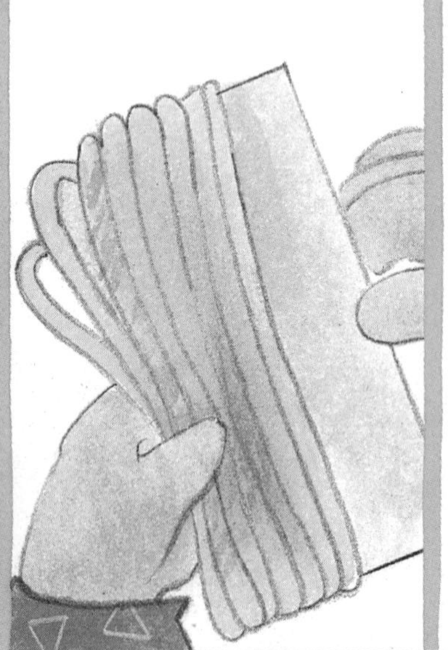

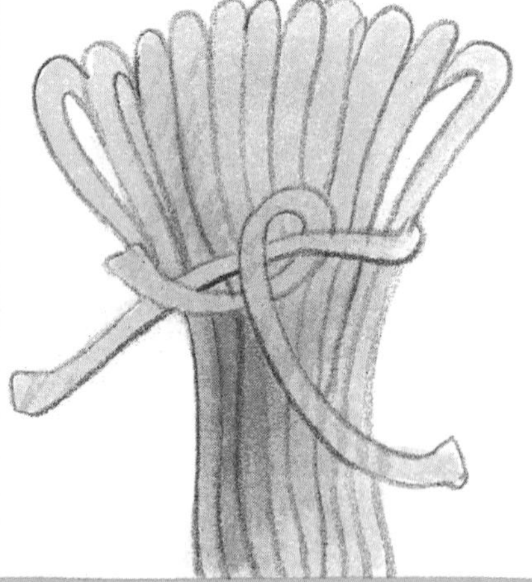

4 Tie another 50cm (20-inch) piece of yarn below the hair to form your doll's head.

5 Cut all the loop ends on the bottom of the doll.

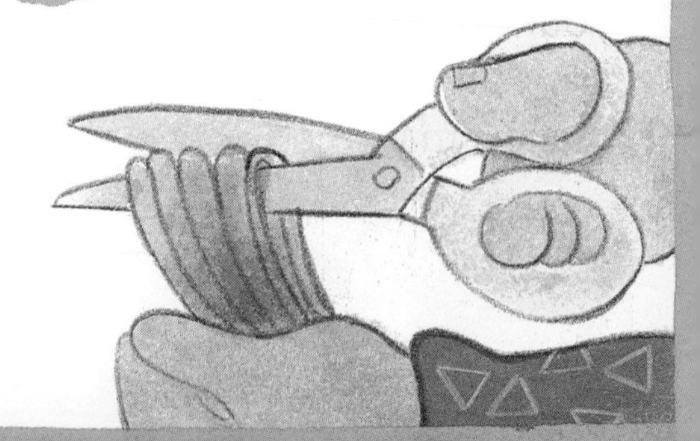

6 Separate some of the strands of yarn from the sides of your doll to make the arms. Tie them with pieces of yarn. Trim off the extra yarn.

7 Tie your doll at the waist with a piece of yarn.

8 Separate the remaining strands into two equal parts to make your doll's legs. Tie them at the feet. Finish your doll with a face.

Fun ideas to try

- If you want your doll to wear a skirt, don't tie it at the feet.
- Braid the arms and legs.
- Tie strings on your doll's head, arms and feet to make a marionette.

OLD-FASHIONED HANKY DOLL

THINGS YOU NEED:

1. Lay the handkerchief flat on the table, right side down.

2. Put some stuffing about the size of your fist a hand's-width down from the top.

3. Use the rubber band to fasten the stuffing in the handkerchief.

4. Tie knots in the top two corners of the handkerchief to make arms.

5. Apply glue in a circle around your doll's face.

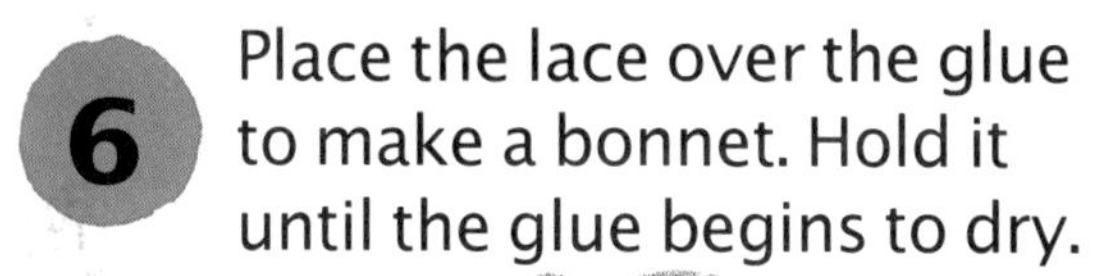

6 Place the lace over the glue to make a bonnet. Hold it until the glue begins to dry.

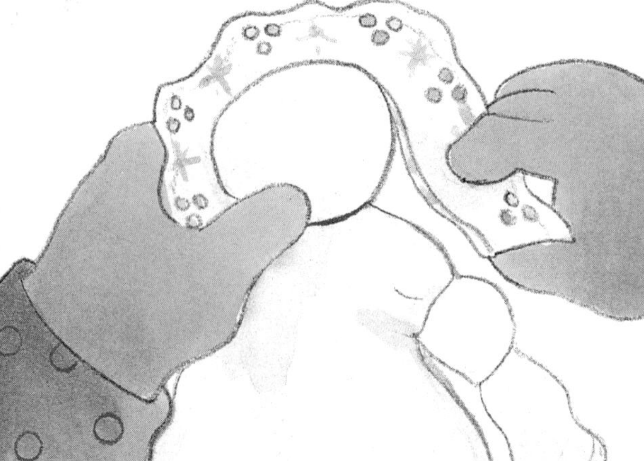

7 Tie the ribbon around the doll's neck to cover the rubber band .

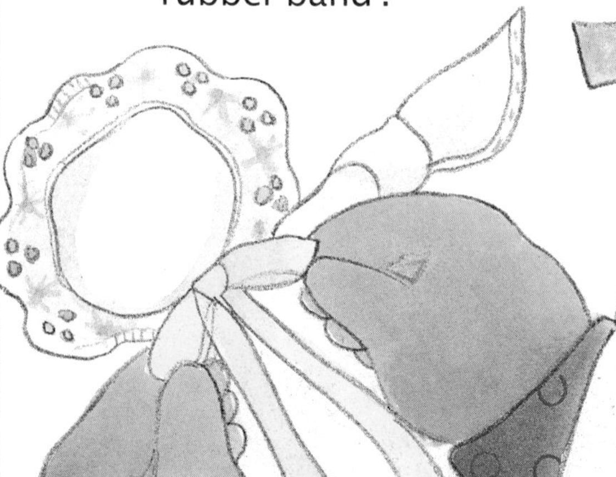

8 Traditionally, a doll like this does not have a face, but give yours one, if you like.

Fun ideas to try

- Make a handkerchief doll out of a colourful bandanna.
- Make legs on your doll by tying knots in the bottom corners, too.

ROLY-POLY DOLLS

THINGS YOU NEED:

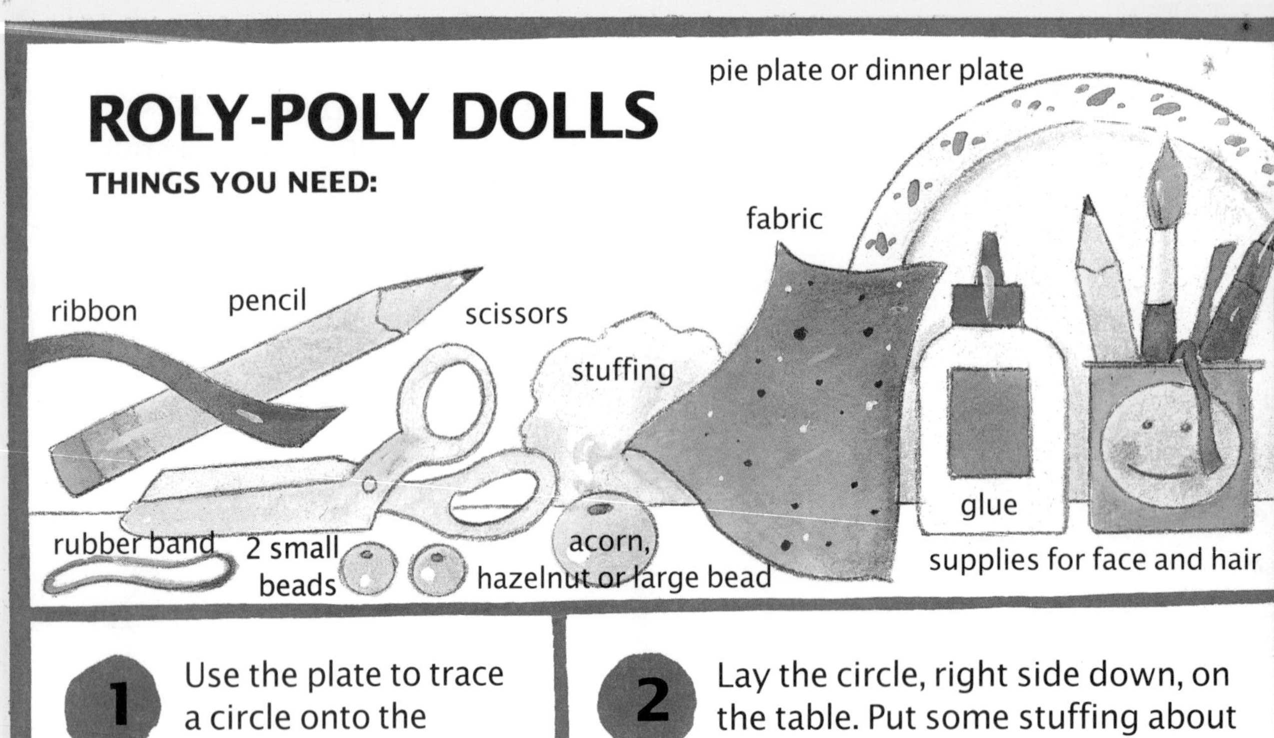

1 Use the plate to trace a circle onto the fabric. Cut it out.

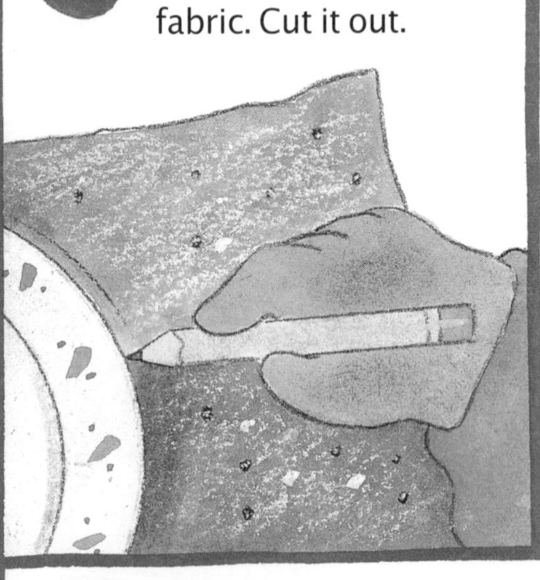

2 Lay the circle, right side down, on the table. Put some stuffing about the size of your fist into the centre of it.

3 Gather the fabric around the stuffing to form a skirt. Use the rubber band to hold it together.

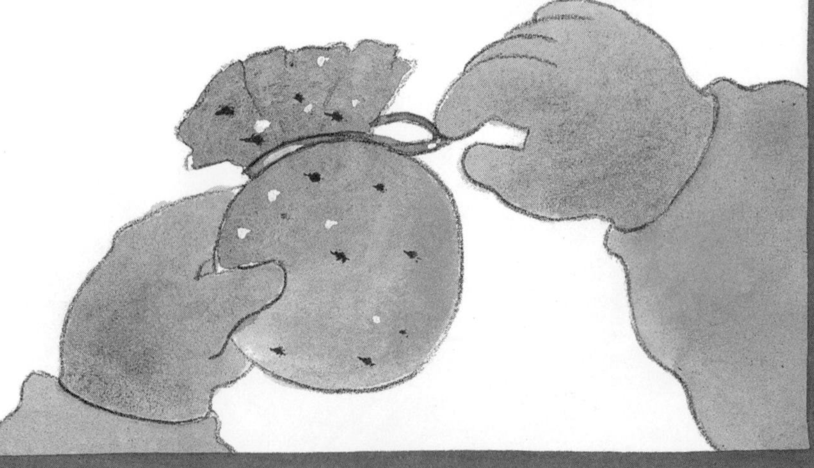

4 Tie the ribbon around your doll's waist, covering the rubber band. Knot it at the back.

5 Thread a small bead onto each ribbon and tie a knot to make arms. Trim any extra ribbon.

6 Squirt glue into the centre of your doll's gathered neck.

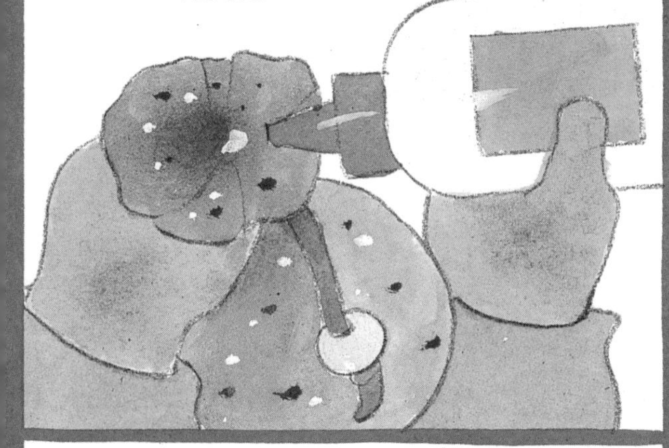

7 Sit your doll's head on this glue. Give it time to dry, then give your doll a face and hairstyle.

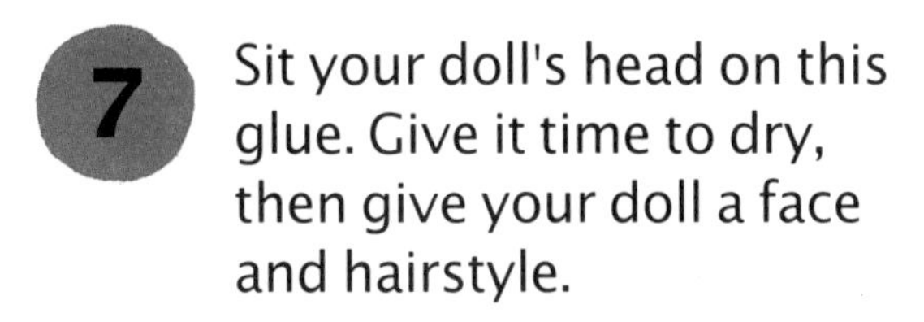

Fun ideas to try

- Sprinkle some potpourri in with the stuffing to make a fragrant doll.
- Use Roly-Poly Doll for a pin cushion. It makes a great gift.

NOODLE NEIGHBOURS

THINGS YOU NEED:

paint (optional)

rigatoni noodle

elbow macaroni

rice

bead for head

glue

supplies for face

1 Glue the bead on top of the rigatoni noodle.

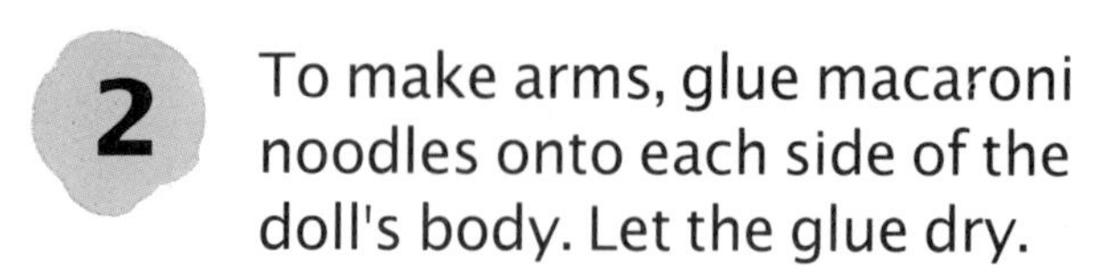

2 To make arms, glue macaroni noodles onto each side of the doll's body. Let the glue dry.

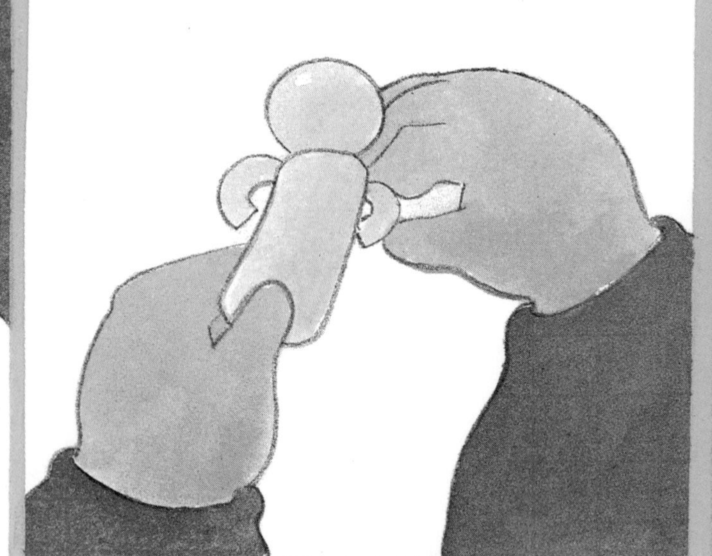

3 If your doll's bead head has a large hole in it, glue a small piece of paper over it. Apply glue all over the top of the doll's head.

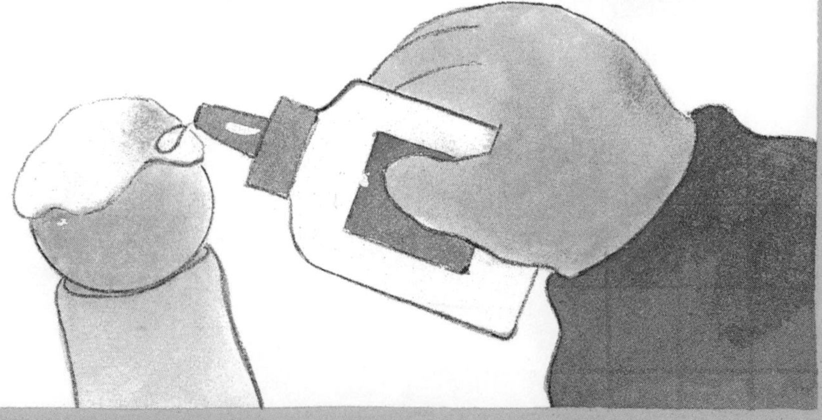

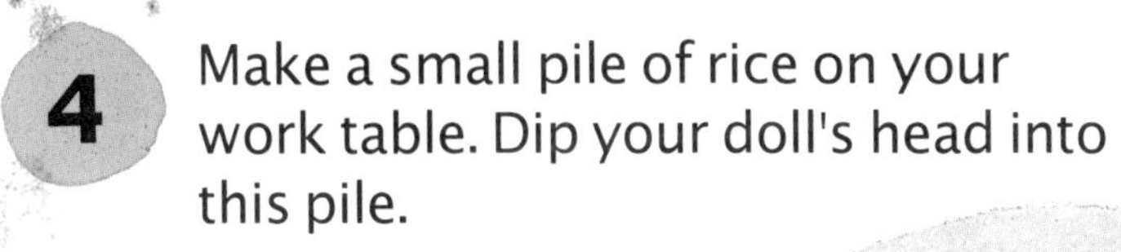

4 Make a small pile of rice on your work table. Dip your doll's head into this pile.

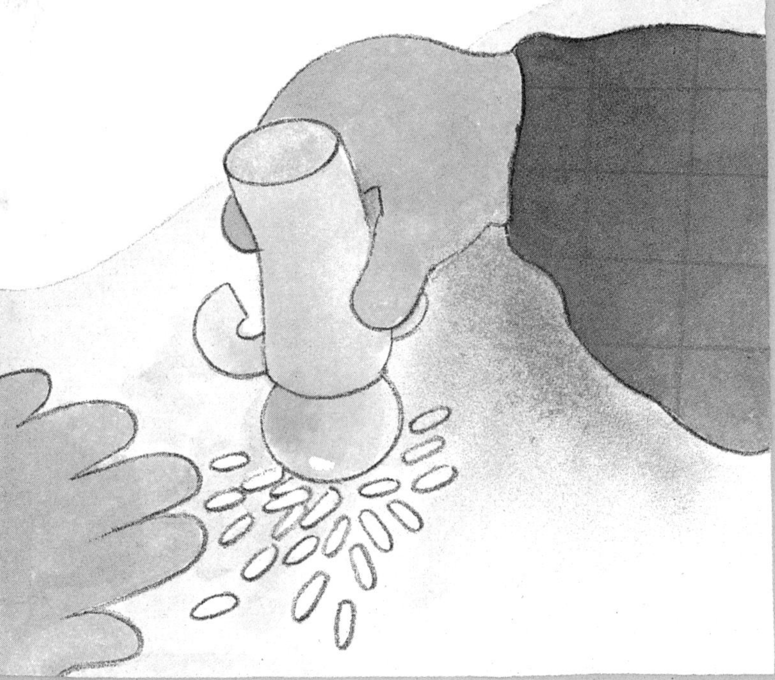

5 If you like, you can paint your doll's body, arms and hair.

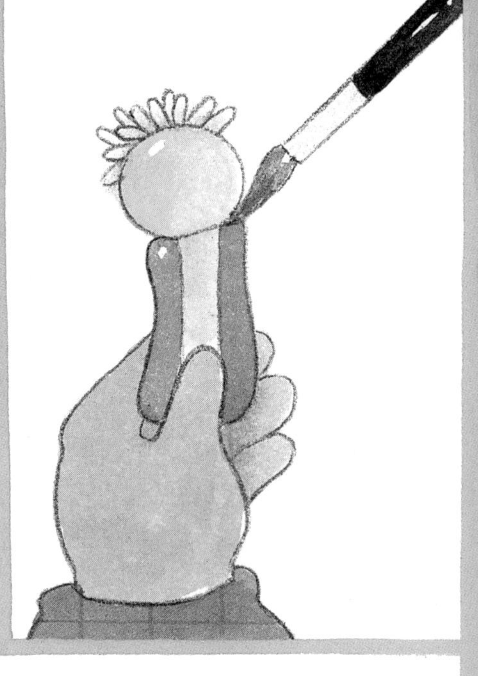

6 Give your noodle neighbour a face.

Fun ideas to try

- Glue a bow-shaped noodle to your doll's back to make an angel.
- Use larger pasta, such as cannelloni noodles and oversized macaroni, for a bigger doll.

MINIATURES

THINGS YOU NEED:

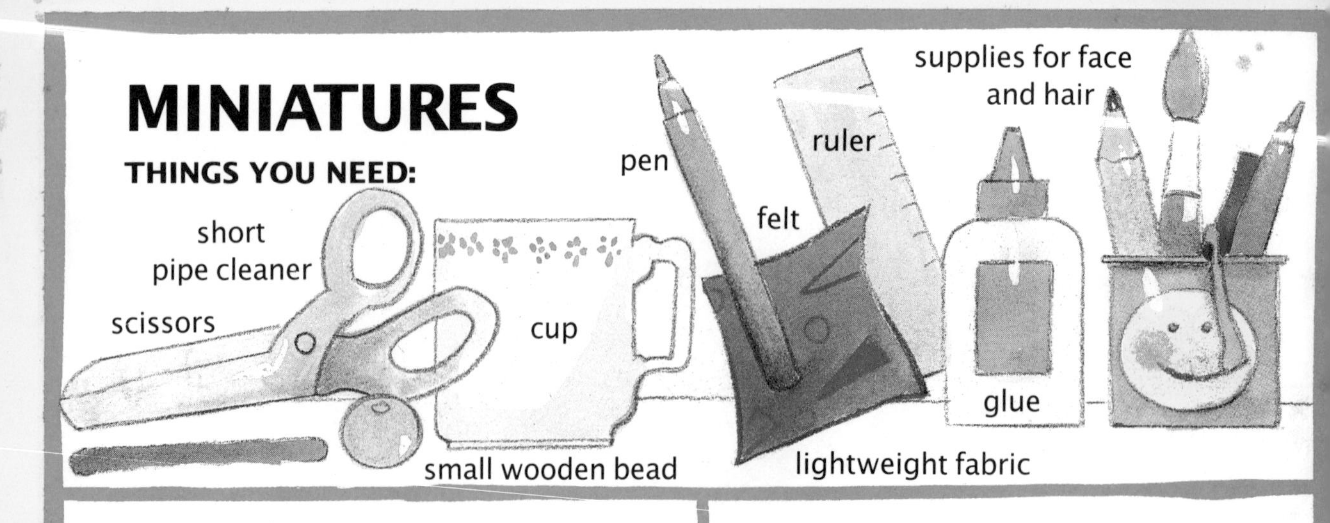

1 Cut a piece of pipe cleaner about 10 cm (4 inches) long. Bend it in half.

2 Use a cup to trace a circle onto the fabric. Cut it out.

3 To find the centre of the fabric circle, fold it in half and then in half again. The peak is the centre. Place this centre over the bent end of the pipe cleaner.

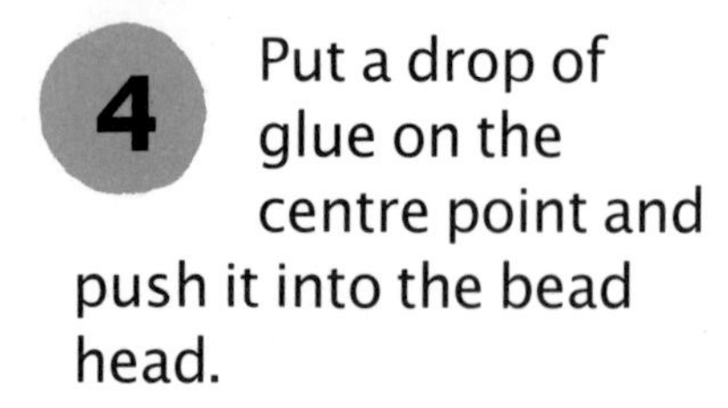

4 Put a drop of glue on the centre point and push it into the bead head.

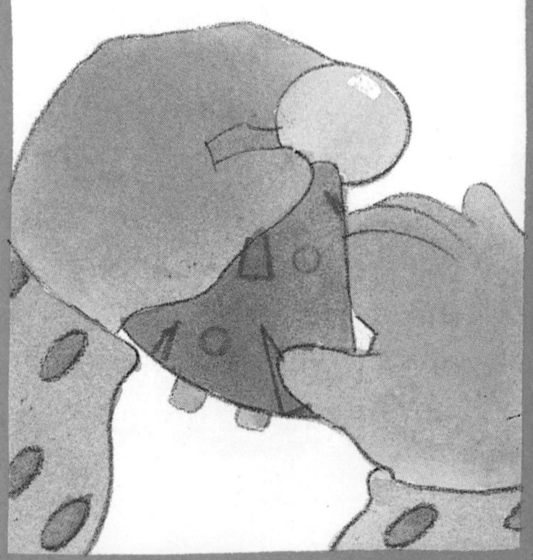

5 Cut a small strip of felt for your doll's shawl.

6 Put glue on one side of the shawl and wrap it around your doll.

7 Your miniature should stand on its own. Trim the dress and bend the pipe cleaners to look like feet. To stiffen the dress and prevent it from fraying, run a line of glue around the edge.

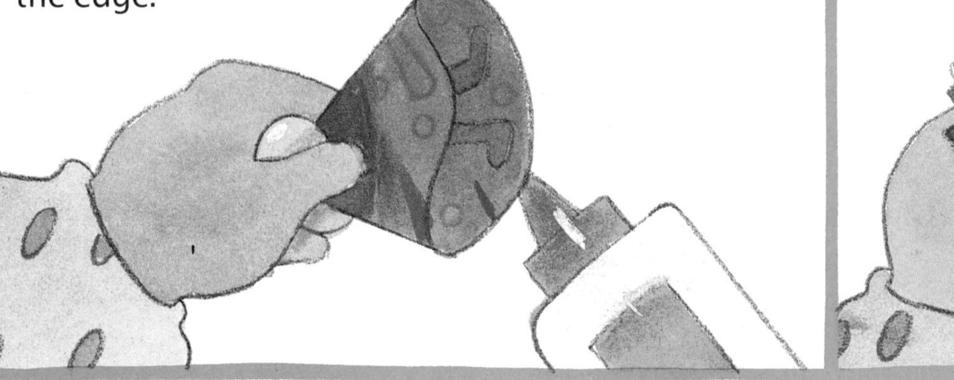

8 Give your doll a face and hairstyle.

Fun ideas to try

★ Make arms for your doll by wrapping a piece of pipe cleaner around to the back, twisting it twice and bringing the "arms" forward. You will not need to glue the shawl on as it can be tucked under the arms.

BENDABLE WORRY DOLLS

THINGS YOU NEED:

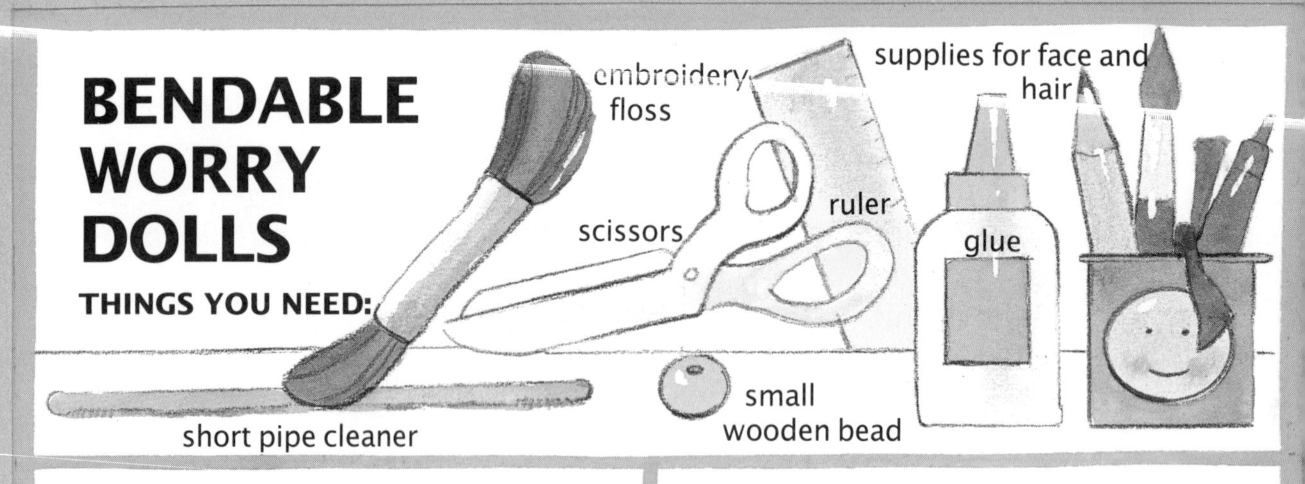

1 Cut the pipe cleaner into two pieces: one about 5 cm (2 inches) and the other about 10 cm (4 inches).

2 Bend the longer piece in half. Put a drop of glue on the bent end and slide it into the bead.

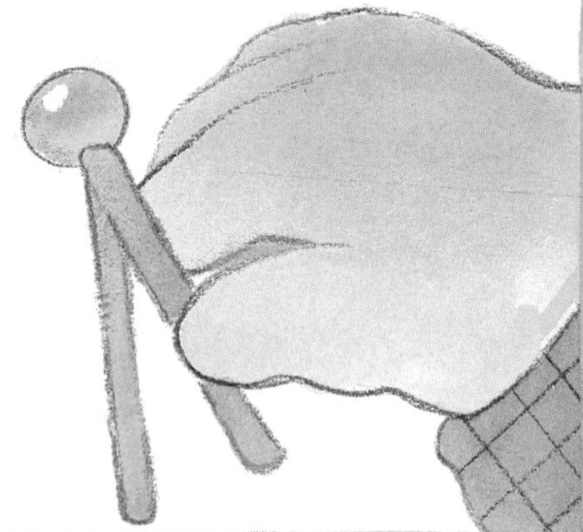

3 Place the short piece across the back of the doubled pipe cleaner, with one side a little longer than the other one. Wrap the longer side around the body and return it to the arm position.

4 Fold the end of each pipe cleaner to look like hands and feet.

5 Place the end of the floss at the neck and along one arm. Begin winding the floss around the arm, starting at the hand. Cover over the floss end.

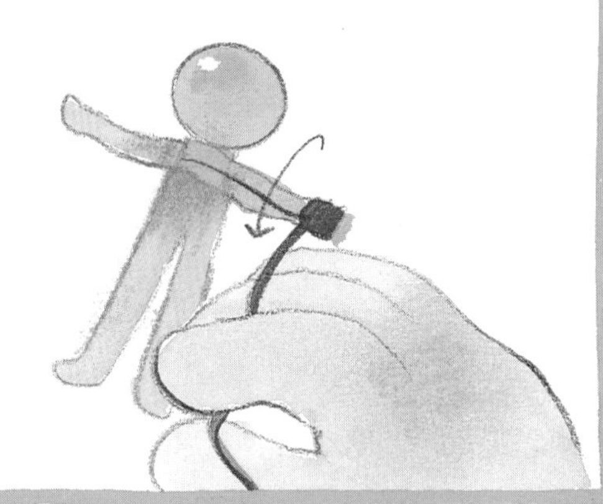

6 Wind across the shoulders to the other arm and back across. Continue to wind down the body. When you reach the legs, wind the floss down one leg, up that leg, down the other leg and up until you are back to the waist.

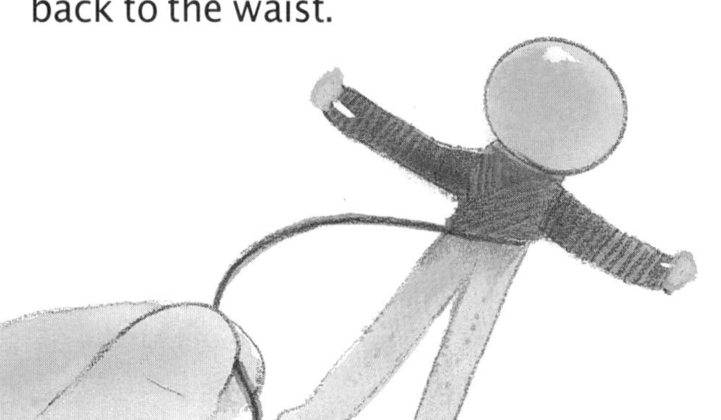

7 Dot some glue onto the back of your doll. Cut off the floss and press it into the glue. Hold it until it begins to dry.

8 Finish your doll with a face and hair.

Fun ideas to try

- Use different colours of floss, to look like clothes. Just remember to glue the ends of each floss piece as you start and finish.
- If you'd like to hang your doll on earrings or a necklace, do not use any glue at step #2. Push the pipe cleaner through the bead so that the bent end sticks out. Use this looped end to attach onto jewellery.

DOLLS GALORE

Now that you've made dozens of dolls, here are some fun things to do with them.

★ Tie or glue a string to your doll. Hang the doll from a doorknob, key chain, zipper or pencil case.

★ Buy undecorated earrings, barrettes and hairbands at a craft supply store. Glue dolls onto them. Pin dolls to your shirt, shoes or hat.

★ Make a whole community of dolls. Include the hockey team, playground kids, construction workers, teachers, grocery clerks and other people in your neighbourhood.

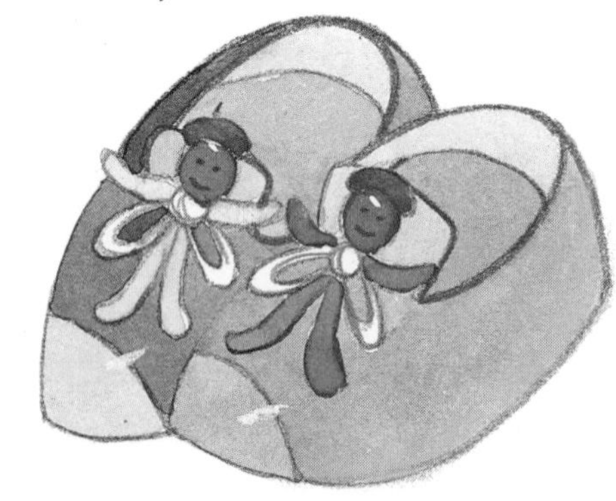

★ Make doll look-alikes of your family and friends.

★ Glue a magnetic strip to your doll and make a fridge magnet.

★ Pose a bendable doll on a mug, picture frame, napkin ring, basket or gift.